3 Stories Book

By
Dennis
Pepper

Table of Contents

Mygoof's Magic Wand

Chapter 1

"Begone with you." These were the excited words of a little four year old boy by the name of Mygoof. They were often heard echoing around the small mining village of Dimble-Wake, a delightful little village of old ramshackle miner's cottages, where everybody knew each other by name.

Mygoof was a cheerful, playful boy, who got up to all kinds of mischief. This was only to be expected, as with all children at the tender age of four years and a bit

Never a day would pass without Mygoof being ticked off for doing something silly or naughty, whereby he would often receive a wagging finger of disapproval. But these wrongs and silliness were only in the eyes of grown-ups, for what would a grown-up know about the delights of jumping in and out of muddy puddles or building mud dams just after it had rained? So he would get himself a little wet and dirty. But then this was Mygoof's world; a dreamers world, it was good fun.

The making of dams was good fun, but Mygoof's greatest love was the mystical art of magic. This interest in magic came about after seeing a magician do some amazing tricks with a pack of playing cards, but within the act the magician made a woman disappear from within a long wooden box, only to bring her back again, this happened only after the magician had waved and tapped the box with the wand and uttering a few wards that Mygoof did not understand.

From that day on, Mygoof was truly smitten with art of magic. Everyday he wore a wizard's cloak that his mother had lovingly made for him. It bore several yellow stars and a large quarter moon that sparkled in the sunlight. She had also made a pointed hat that bent over at its tip. But after a short while Mygoof refused to wear the hat, this was after his friends laughed at him, as did others in the village. They were not poking fun at Mygoof; it was simply that he looked so comical. But nevertheless, he refused to wear the hat, for he thought he looked more like a witch than a magician.

The village band-master, Mr Tuneful, and Mygoof's father were very good friends. On seeing Mygoof playing with a stick as a wand, Mr Tuneful gave Mygoof's father one of his old conductor batons for Mygoof to play with.

On giving baton to Mygoof, his father told him, that it had once belonged to a wise and powerful old magician. He also told Mygoof that the magician had admitted to him that the power in the old wand seemed to have faded and at times would not work too well or obey his commands. It was then that the wise old magician decided to replace it with a new and more powerful wand from the great chief of all the wizards.

"Is there such a person?" asked Mygoof, wanting to know more about him.

"Of cause, there is always someone in charge, I believe the chief magician is called, The Archimage, but he is such a private person that he never sees anyone, that is unless he knows them and they call upon his help. The old wise magician also insisted that because the old wand still had much unreliable power left in it, you should take great care of it." said his father. And this Mygoof promised to do.

With his magician's wand in hand, Mygoof was often seen in the village tapping two or three times on almost everything, whilst yelling joyfully, "Be gone with you."

Looking skywards, he would shout and wave his wand at passing clouds that momentarily blocked the sun, 'Be gone with you,' and the rays of light once again burst out from behind the clouds, thus giving those watching him at play very much pleasure.

Mygoof was very lucky for he lived in a house near the top of a hill and from his bedroom window he could see below much of the mining village and the entrance to the mine and beyond that a very large expanse of water called Dragoon Lake. But the local fisherman called the lake 'Dragon's lake.'

Dragoon Lake was so wide that only on a clear day could Mygoof sees the other side. It was just as well, as some of his friends said that on the other side of the lake lived a group of fire breathing dragons that cooked and ate anyone caught near their shore.

Mygoof knew better than to believe these tales, for he had seen fisher men in boats venture onto the lake and later had seen them return. But still, Mygoof had no desire to ever venture onto the lake, for the waters of the lake were dark and very deep and he certainly did not want to go to the other side to see or find for himself any fire breathing dragons.

Even at his age Mygoof was wise enough to know that such things as dragons did not exist. He vaguely remembered a story his father had told him about, 'George and the dragon,' where the dragon was slain by George, but he doubted it would have been a fire eating dragon. He knew that these stories were told by the fisher men and parents alike to scare children away from the lake. But he did wonder sometimes if these creatures might still exist, for he had also heard stories about the Loch Ness Monster in Scotland. Some people believe and claimed that they had seen it.

These thoughts often came to mind whilst looking out over the still dark waters where his imagination would run amuck. 'Who knows what lurks in the depths of these waters other than small fish, eels and a few croaking frogs,' But he had no intention of ever finding out, for it was also said that the mist floating over the lake first thing in the morning was the steam from the dragon's fiery breath, and with this foolish thought in mind he could not help but laugh to himself.

Chapter 2

The coal mine where Mygoof's father worked sat at the edge of the village and could be seen from Mygoof's bedroom window. It was adrift mine that had one entrance sloping into a large cavernous hole cut into the side of a hill.

There was no large lifting machinery to haul coal and heavy tools in and out of the mine other than coal wagons. Instead, miners walked to and from the entrance, carrying what equipment they needed that day, including their lunch-boxes.

Some of the men entering the mine would sneakily hold back wagons on rails, load themselves and tools, then release the breaks and run noisily clattering down the slope into the mine.

Miners trudged out of the mine with blackened faces. Some miners with stooped back would slowly and wearily clamber up the hill towards the village after first stopping outside the entrance to stretch their aching backs whilst filling their lungs with the cool fresh air that came in off the lake. Then each man would turn off the lights on their hard hats that now flickered dimly in the sunlight before placing them on a bench to be recharged.

As the miners ambled slowly down the slope there seemed to be only gloom on their solemn faces. There was little or no happiness here. No one spoke or smiled. At times, a miner would turn and wave to someone upon the hill and in turn a wife or child would wave back as though they might be watching their loved ones entering the black gaping mouth of the 'Devil' for the last time.

During the day while the children were at school the village was very quiet, it was only when the children were let out to play at break times that the eerie calm was broken.

Mygoof, who wasn't yet old enough to go to school was forced to play alone, but he found that there was always something to do to amuse himself.

He was often seen by villagers teasing spiders by lightly tickling their cobwebs with his wand and watching the spider dart from its lair in the hope of finding a meal trapped within its fine silky web, only to scurry back disappointed when it found its trap empty. If it had recently rained the spiders would be left in peace, for then puddles and making dams were Mygoof's joy.

Mygoof would then break dams open sending water cascading from one to the other.

But even though Mygoof's day was full of fun he still longed to be able to go to school with most of his older friends.

Mygoof strolled aimlessly about the village tapping most things with his little magic wand, he would tap the stems of flowers that were already passed their best and were dying. He would close his eyes then utter the words. "Be gone with you." And when the petals fell to the ground he would cry out with joy. "That's magic."

He tapped almost everything, dogs and cats would cower and scurry off for cover when they were about to be tapped, they would run away and hide. "That's magic." Mygoof would shout as they ran off, their tail between their legs.

Later that day Mygoof's father was watering the garden with a sprinkler hose on seeing Mygoof tested out his magician's wand by trying to stop the water from the hose. Mygoof would tap two or three times the nozzle of the hose and demand it to stop or start.

Unseen by Mygoof, his father decided to play a joke on him by turning the tap on and off at Mygoof's command.

Mygoof went off believing that there was indeed a lot of power left in the wand and he would need to be very careful as to where and how he used it, but he also realized that sometimes it did not work so well, he now understood why the magician did not want it anymore.

Whilst sitting at the dinner table that day Mygoof asked his father about it, for he thought that he was doing or saying something wrong.

"Why doesn't my wand always work?" he asked sadly.

"I really don't know. Maybe magic wands are like people, they get tired and need time to rest. They need to rebuild their strength and energy."

"If you over-work anything, it will soon wear out. Do you ever get tired?"

"Yes, of course I do." Mygoof replied.

"And when you have rested or had a good nights sleep, do you feel refreshed?"

"Yes, Of course I do."

Mygoof's father pulled a wry face and raised his eyebrows. "Well, there you go then."

Believing this to be the reason for failure, Mygoof would in future go on to choose his subjects more carefully when working his magic.

Chapter 3

Some days later, on another hill in the village, a miner by the name of Jimmy Seymore was sat at his breakfast-table eating a hearty meal before setting off to work at the mine. It was this very morning that his beautiful wife, Sue, had told him that they were now going to have their first child. This was such a surprise to Jimmy that he had spilt his tea with shock before laughing and hugging his wife joyously.

Jimmy and Sue had been married many years and had longed for a child of their own, but had yet to have been blessed with one.

Sue had made Jimmy a fresh cup of tea, and whilst Jimmy drank it, they debated over what name they should name their unborn child.

Sue decided that if it was to be a girl, then the name should be Dolcy after her mother. Jimmy wanted, if blessed with a boy, then the child should bear his father's middle name of Wallace. They were both happy with their chosen names and hugged each other tenderly before Jimmy went happily off to work.

Jimmy had never been so happy as he was that morning while walking to the mine's entrance, waving and throwing silent kisses to Sue until he was out of sight in the 'Devils' mouth.

His friends had remarked on his happy mood, they all wanted to know the reason why, but Jimmy never told them, for he was not one for counting his chickens before they hatched, and he would say nothing until it was certain that the baby was in mother's arms. To his surprise, Jimmy had found that this morning the mine seemed extremely cold and damp.

Outside, despite being a sunny day and good news that Sue had given him, he now felt glum by having to go deep into the mine and on to the coal face some distance from the entrance.

Like a bad omen, Jimmy shivered as though a cold wind had cooled him to the bone, but he shrugged it off as just a bad feeling of having left a happy wife and a sunny day outside, for a gloomy dusty darkness of the mine.

The coal face where the miners were working that day was a good ten minute's walk down towards the lake, where water would be forever dripping from the overhead roof props that often creaked loudly with the weight of rock upon them. When heard these loud creaks would cause a flurry of alarm amongst the miners, as they rushed to reinforce the creaking prop with extra wood support.

Jimmy was working with eight other miners on the coal face on that day, but not much was said between them while walking and carrying picks and shovels towards their designated work place and by the time they had reached the coal face sweat was already flowing from their brows. Their shoulders and backs would be aching from having to stoop owing to the roof of the mine being so low. Breathing was also hard through poor ventilation, making the air dank and full of coal-dust.

Meanwhile outside the mine, the village was bathed in bright sunlight, bringing smiles to villagers' faces. Being a close community, nearly everyone in the village knew each other by name, and children were safe to walk freely within the village, as long as their parents knew where they were or where they were going.

So Mygoof and his antics were endured and seen upon as a form of entertainment, for everybody knew the whereabouts of Mygoof, by the tapping of his wand and the utterance of, "Be gone with you."

Chapter 4

Down at the lake was an old stone jetty that was lined on each side with railings; this stopped anyone accidentally falling in. The jetty jutted some distance out onto the dark waters, where, on days like this, miners would sit for hours on end, fishing, not that they ever caught anything. They went there just to relax whilst breathing in the cool dust-free air that rolled in across the vast expanse of water.

Once in a while, there would be a hushed murmur from the men as someone would be lucky enough to have caught a fish. After releasing the fish from the hook they would throw it back in.

Sometime ago, whilst venturing onto the jetty with his father, Mygoof had discovered an old metal pipe sticking out of it. It was rusting and looked as old as the jetty itself, Mygoof had no idea as to why it was there, nor did his father.

It was so peaceful here on the jetty that the men fishing did not speak to each other very much, or if they did, they would speak in whispers. The only time anyone ever said anything loudly was to jokingly say to Mygoof. "Begone with you." They would then chuckle and laugh amongst themselves.

Chapter 5

The very morning that Jimmy Seymore found out that he was going to be a father, Mygoof decided to go to the pier. It was a hot day, very hot and humid.

On passing the entrance of the mine, Mygoof felt a sudden tremble underfoot and thought he heard the distant rumble of thunder, though the sky was clear of any clouds. Glancing at the mine's gaping entrance, he saw what he thought were little splutters of dust stream out of the darkened soil as though large drips of rain had just fallen onto it.

"Be gone with you." Mygoof said, waving his wand at the entrance.

No sooner had he said the magical words, when there was a loud rumbling sound and the earth shuddered and shook, throwing him off balance and to the ground. As he stared at the gaping hole of the Devil's mouth, it was suddenly engulfed in a black cloud of dust that billowed from its entrance, as though it was being violently sick whilst the side of the hill above the entrance slid down, covering it in earth.

The entrance and the mine had gone, it had totally disappeared.

Mygoof sat in shocked disbelief. He could not believe what had just happened. "How is this possible?" he asked himself aloud, looking at the wand. "No, no, I didn't mean it, please undo the spell." Mygoof cried with all urgency to his little wand, horrified as to what had just happened. "I really didn't mean it. Undo the spell." He yelled and frantically waving the wand at the hill where the entrance had once been.

Mygoof had never tried so hard to undo a spell before, and no matter how much he pleaded with the wand, nothing happened. He could not understand how his little magic wand could have become powerful enough to do so much damage. He now thought that may be he had rested it far too long. Shouting at the top of his voice he called out to the unseen Archimage for help, to come and undo the spell, but no matter how much he pleaded, the great wizard never responded.

While this happened, mayhem broke loose in the village. There was the sound of slapping of wood upon wood, the clanging of metal on metal, hoots and whistles blew, as people ran in all directions trying to raise the alarm in any which way they could as they mustered up help for the poor miners that were now trapped within the mine.

Mygoof's father was not at work the day of the accident. Without another look towards the mine, Mygoof ran home passing his father coming the other way towards the mine. Mygoof tried to stop him. "Not now Mygoof, the mines collapsed. "he yelled rushing by without stopping.

Mygoof tried to explain to his mother that he did not really want the mine destroyed, it was an accident.

Mygoof's mother couldn't understand a word of what he was saying until she had calmed him down by hugging him gently on her lap.

"You silly little wizard," she said tenderly wiping away his tears with her pinafore. "It wasn't you, or your magic wand. It must have been a small tremor that caused a landslide."

He did not believe it was as simple as an earth tremor. It must have been his magic wand. Even though his mother had reassured Mygoof that it was not his fault, he still believed that his wand had caused the landslide.

Chapter 6

Three days passed and not one miner had yet been rescued from the mine. There had also been no contact with them, and every one feared the worst.

Mygoof's father went to the mine every day to help in the rescue of men trapped and entombed or missing far below ground.

Everybody in the village was very worried and concerned about the trapped miners. They were now frantic with worry for they had not heard anything from them. They did not know if miners had survived the cave-in, and if they had, where were they trapped? It was also felt that if they survived their food and water would be running out.

Mygoof wearily ventured back out onto the jetty. There were no fishermen there to be seen as Mygoof walked slowly to the far end of the jetty to where the rusty old metal pipe protruded from it.

He planned to rid himself of what he believed the cause of the accident, still believing that his little wand was responsible for the miner's plight.

It was now time for the wand 'to be gone.' And no one else should have its powers.

Reaching the rusty old pipe, Mygoof put his hand into his cloak pocket and removed his beloved magician's wand, intending to throw it as far as he could out into the lake. He felt extremely saddened for the trapped miners, but also for the fact that he needed to rid himself of the only real treasure that he had ever had.

Without thinking he struck the pipe twice and uttered in an angry voice, "Be gone with you." He demanded as though the pipe had somehow got in his way.

Fascinated by what followed, for the sound of his two taps came back out of the pipe. Mygoof tapped three more times on the pipe and of course the sounds of his three taps came back. He tapped four times more, again four taps came back. He decided this is some kind of magic; he would tap twice, pause then tap three more times. Again the taps returned, but this time only with three taps.

Mygoof realized that what he was hearing must be an echo. "Hello," he shouted into the pipe, expecting the echo of his own voice to come back, but it was not the sound of his voice that returned.

"Hello..., is that you Mygoof?"

'It's the great wizard, the Archimage." Thought Mygoof. He did not wait around to play with the pipe anymore, for the voice he had just heard could be Archimage's. Thinking to himself that the great wizard would be angry with him in wanting to rid himself of magic wand.

But before he had gone ten yards he suddenly realized he may have just had heard the voice of the trapped miners.

He needed to get help quickly but still there were no fishermen on the jetty that Mygoof could tell.

Running home as fast as he could Mygoof tried to explain to his mother and father what had happened at the pipe. They laughed and told him it was just an echo. But Mygoof insisted it was the miners.

His father was very tired after working so hard looking for the miners. He would have listened to him in ordinary circumstances but he had no time for Mygoof's childish imagination and made this feeling known to Mygoof by telling him off. He was sent to his bedroom and only come out when his dinner was ready.

"Why won't any one believe me?" He cried as he obeyed his father and made his way to his room.

After dinner, Mygoof made his way back to the jetty. Still there were no fishermen to be seen before he reached the old pipe. He tapped the pipe three times with his wand and waited, but before he could tap again a voice said,

"Is that you Mygoof?"

"Yes." Mygoof replied.

"Who are you?"

"I'm Jimmy Seymore." Then there was a pause.

"Can you still hear me Mygoof?"

"Yes I can still hear you." Mygoof replied, unsure of himself.

"Where are you?"

"I'm in the old disused part of mine with the other miners. There's been a heavy rock fall behind us and we are trapped with no other means of escape."

There was another pause before Jimmy said. "We're all safe so far, but the only source of air is the pipe I am talking to you through. Now please, be gone with you and go and tell your father where we are."

"I've already tried, but he doesn't believe me." Mygoof explained.

"Then you must try again Mygoof." Said Jimmy, despair in his voice. "Tell him it's me, and pull him by the hand if you have too, but get someone here as quickly as you can."

Again, Mygoof wasted no time. He looked for the fishermen on the jetty but they were no where to be seen. He ran the whole length of the jetty never stopping to catch his breath. The first person he saw was a miner called Troy Wilks. Troy was an over sized giant of a man.

"Mr Wilks, Mr Wilks." Mygoof shouted panting heavily.

Mr Wilks was dirty and looked extremely tired as he slowly clambered up the steep hill leading from the mine. His face was caked with coal dust and was heavily streaked with sweat. Troy Wilks stopped and stood there glaring down at Mygoof with red blood shot tired eyes.

"Mr Wilks, I have just been speaking to Jimmy Seymore and...." Mygoof did not get the chance to finish what he was saying before Mr Wilks glared down at Mygoof and said in an unfriendly tone of voice.

"Be gone with you Mygoof and go play your silly games elsewhere, I have no time now for this tomfoolery. Be gone with you!"

"But..." retorted Mygoof, taking hold of Mr Wilks dirty jacket sleeve, intending to pull the big man and lead him to the jetty.

"Be gone with you I say Mygoof." Said Mr Wilks angrily, shrugging Mygoof aside.

Next person he met was Mr Daily, the mine's watchman, tall slim and speckled man who always wear a waist coat with a watch chain clasped to his pocket. But again Mr Daily gently pushed him aside, telling him "Be gone with you."

This sort of thing happened repeatedly. No one believed him. He was forever being told to, "Be gone with you." For they had other things on their minds and they were all too worried for the miners to be distracted.

Feeling rejected, Mygoof hurried back to the old pipe, still there was no one on the jetty fishing.

Mygoof relayed to Jimmy Seymore what had happened and said that he was sorry he could not get anyone to believe him.

"Do you know my wife Sue?" Jimmy asked.

"Yes, of course I know her." Mygoof replied.

"Good, then go and tell her that you have been speaking with me." Jimmy instructed.

"What if she doesn't believe me?" Mygoof queried.

Tell her that the name of our child-to-be will be called, Dolcy or Wallace."

"Dolcy or Wallace, is that it?" Mygoof asked.

"Yes, that's it, Dolcy or Wallace. Now hurry." Instructed Jimmy, "The air down here is getting a little hard to breathe."

Once again, Mygoof made his way back along the jetty. After running around all day, he found climbing the hill to Jimmy Seymore's house very hard going, this was something he had never noticed before. By the time he had reached Jimmy Seymore's house, he was nearly on his knees with exhaustion.

Mygoof stretched up to the door-knocker and banged hard upon it. No sooner had he removed his hand from the knocker than the door hastily sprung open.

Sue Seymore stood there as though she had been expecting someone else, disappointment showing on her pretty face as she looked down and recognized Mygoof.

"Not now Mygoof, please, be gone with you." She pleaded.

"Please Mrs Seymore! I've been speaking with Mr Seymore."

"I told you, not now Mygoof, please. Be gone with you." Sue repeated angrily. "Go and do your magic elsewhere." She insisted and abruptly closed the door on him.

"Jimmy said the child would be called Dolcy or Wallace." Mygoof shouted through the letter-box.

Suddenly the door sprang open. With unexpected speed Sue bent down and grabbed hold of Mygoof by the arms. Her grip very was strong but Mygoof did not flinch for he had realized that she now believed him. "Where is he?" Take me to him, quickly." She demanded, grabbing hold of Mygoof's hand.

Mygoof wasted no time leading Sue back down the hill to the jetty and towards the old rusty pipe.

"Where on earth are we going Mygoof?" she asked as they scurried along the deserted jetty.

"They're at the end of the jetty in the pipe." Mygoof said.

On hearing that they were in the pipe Sue suddenly stopped, halting Mygoof at the same time. She looked down at Mygoof with doubt plastered on her face and asked. "This isn't one of your silly little games is it Mygoof? You haven't been secretly listening to people's conversations have you?"

"No, truly, they are down the pipe, you can talk to them." Mygoof replied pulling at her hand.

On reaching the pipe Mygoof extracted his wand and struck the pipe three times.

"Hello, is that you Mygoof?" Came back the voice.

Sue instantly recognized Jimmy's voice, though it was distorted from travelling through the pipe.

"Jimmy it's me, Sue." Sue said bursting into relieved tears of happiness.

"How can we help?"

"Tell the rescue team to dig down through the jetty. "Jimmy informed her" We are not too far down, but we haven't the tools to get ourselves out."

Sue was gone in a flash to get the rescue team, leaving Mygoof to keep the miners company.

As he waited for her to return a mist started to descend upon the jetty. This was now making Mygoof very nervous.

His imagination was starting to work overtime as he looked out over the dark waters of the lake from where the mist was rolling in. Occasionally he heard the splash of a fish or frog making him jump.

'Or was that one of the dragons dropping its bar of soap?' He asked himself.

It seemed like hours, not minutes that had passed since Sue had left him alone.

Far off, Mygoof heard the sound of excited voices and the clanking of metal tools. Looking at the village he saw a mass of men coming towards him carrying picks and shovels.

The first man on the scene was Mr Wilks, followed closely by Mygoof's father. Bending down Mr Wilks lifted Mygoof up and gave him a big hug. "Well done Mygoof, you clever little wizard. I will never doubt the wonders of your magic wand again." He said gently putting him down.

Mygoof's father just stood there staring at him and shaking his head before stooping down and taking him up in to his arms. "I too will never doubt you again my son." He said, tears flowing from his eyes as he gently hugged him.

The hole that the rescue team had dug was quite big, and after putting down a ladder the last person to emerge from it was Jimmy Seymore. He was weak from hunger and very thirsty but he managed to hug his pretty wife, and one by one shake the hands of rescuers. He then looked around and asked. "Where is that little imp Mygoof?"

Mygoof was pointed out by one of the rescuers. "There's that little wizard." He exclaimed smiling.

Mygoof's clothing was now as black and dirty as Mr Wilks and his father were, but that didn't matter. Everyone was overjoyed that the miners were now safe.

Jimmy Seymore hobbled over to Mygoof, and kneeling down he gave him a big hug and kissed him on the cheek.

"I hope I have a son, and when I do, I hope he grows up to be just like you, and I will name him after you. I will call him...," thinking for a moment or two he said. "My son Wallace."

And what if your son should happen to be a girl?" Sue asked laughing.

"Then we should name her..." he said, once again pausing. "My girl Dolcy." He laughed.

Sue now knelt down and gave Mygoof another hug and kiss.

"But you Mygoof, you will forever be My hero." Sue said, taking hold of his hand and walking him home. He needed to prepare for the party the villagers were giving that night, where Mygoof was to be guest of honour. But no magic tricks, they insisted.

They never reopened the mine from that day. Instead, they placed a monument and plaque in the shape of a wand supported by a miners pick in front of it, and inscribed on the plaque was a message that read;

'This plaque is dedicated to a little boy's belief in the wonders of magic. Now begone with you'

© Dennis Pepper

Alexander's Money Tree (Monetary)

Chapter 1

Even though I'm getting old and exercise has become a chore, something happened the other day that suddenly made me remember this story.

It was whilst walking leisurely through the park, working off my lunch and minding my own business, when something hit me on the head. It wasn't a hard, crushing blow like falling of an acorn or I dread to think, the droppings of a bird. But whatever it was, I heard it hit the ground after bouncing off my bald spot and shoulder. I looked up at first expecting to see a large perched bird, or of one flying away. But no, no bird, no squirrel, or anything of interest at all. I then looked down and instantly noticed a brightly new shiny five pence piece, just lying there waiting for me to pick it up. With ageing and aching bones, I bent down, and with unsteady fingers I picked it up and swiftly tucked it in my pocket as though someone may challenge me for it.

"My lucky day." I thought, smiling whilst looking for more. This in turn brought another memory to the forefront of my mind.

I vaguely recall it was last summer, or the summer before that perhaps... anyway I do remember my grandson and I were playing in his garden when he suddenly noticed and picked up a coin that was laying on the freshly mown lawn. I thought at first it was a metal washer that had fallen off the lawn mower, but then upon closer inspection, it proved to be a ten pence coin.

"That's lucky," I told him, watching as he carefully slid it deep into his pocket. Finding this coin seemed to have set off what I could only describe as a treasure hunt, an inquisitive frenzy, of searching in the hope of there being more.

"Come on, Granddad, start looking for more coins," he pleaded excitedly.

'Strange,' I thought. 'At his age he already had a grasp of what money was.' But from where it came, he hadn't a clue, and finding it made it all the more exciting.

"Wow." Was the excited voice of Alexander as he found another coin, then low and-behold, there was another, a bigger and brighter coin, a fifty pence piece, and yet another coin was to be found. But alas this time we were both disappointed, it was only a two pence piece, but money is still money, and no sooner was it in Alexander's hand before it found its way into his pocket.

It suddenly occurred to Alexander that someone must have lost these coins from their pockets whilst lying on the grass, but nevertheless, he was excited by the thought of treasure hunting and started the search for more coins. It was then that Alexander saw what he thought was a silver coin wedged down in what I can only describe as a crack or crevice in the dry sun-baked soil. That day he must have had eyes of a hawk, for I never saw it, even when he pointed it out to me, but sure enough it was there. This coin was wedged tight and within our reach but would be difficult to pick it out with just our fingers.

"We will need a tool to retrieve this one, Alexander." I told him.

"I'll go and get a garden fork from the shed." he said starting to scurry away.

"No, no, just a moment Alexander, we don't want to go digging up daddy's lawn. That would be like taking a sledgehammer to crack a nut. All we need is a twig or stick to prise it free.".

"Good idea, Granddad."

"Yes, my boy, for what you see on my shoulders isn't all dead-wood." I told him tapping the side of my head with two fingers.

Having said that, I found just what we needed, a short but sturdy twig resting amongst his mother's herb garden. I gave it to Alexander, thus bestowing on him the honour and pleasure of retrieving the coin himself whilst I watched as he poked and prodded with frustration. Eventually he retrieved what we thought it was, a five pence piece. It seemed a lot of effort for such a small reward, but as said, money is money and it was soon in Alexander's pocket.

But the search wasn't over just yet, for many more coins were to be discovered. So many coins were found and loaded into Alexander's trouser pockets that eventually he had to hold them up with one hand, or the weight of the coins would have brought them down to his ankles. Our search only came to an end when no more coins were to be found. No matter how hard we searched.

"Nearly time for lunch Alexander, we can always come and search later. "I told him.

Walking back towards the open patio door Alexander suddenly asked. "By the way Granddad, what is a sledgehammer? Is it a tool they use to make snow sledges with? If so, I don't think daddy has one of those."

Emphasizing what I was about to say by taking off my cap and scratching what was the bald patch on top of my head as though in deep thought, I simply replied jokingly, 'Yes I believe that's what they are. But mind you, it would only be for the big ones. In fact, they are large heavy hammers."

Chapter 2

At the beginning of July that year, the days were hot and dry, so after a cool glass of water, Alexander and I decided to have an afternoon nap. I don't know about Alexander but I was extremely tired and fell asleep in the living room armchair.

After our two-hour nap and a bite of late lunch, Alexander and I went back to the garden to play, but our game came to an abrupt end when we looked upon our treasure spot on the lawn and once again discovered load of scattered coins piled and scattered in much the same place as before. It was most odd because, for as far as Alexander knew, no one had been outside since we had gone in and taken our midday nap.

"You know what Alexander?" I said.

"What Granddad?" he asked, not bothering to look up whilst scooping up coins.

"I think we are standing under a money tree." I told him.

"What, a money tree?" he laughed. "Are there such things as money trees. Granddad?" he asked with a question of doubt plastered on his face as he looked up at me.

"Sure, there are, why shouldn't there be? There are all sorts of trees, ash trees, that aren't burnt, rubber trees that can't bend, beech and bay trees without sand or sea. I think any tree is possible." I told him making a play on words. There are also lavatories, but they are hard to grow and just as hard to find when you need one.

"Lavatories? Now I know you're joking Granddad. But money doesn't grow on trees." Alexander argued with a quizzical look.

"I wouldn't count on that, ask your Grandmother, she thinks it does."

'We'll see about that." shouted Grandmother who had been listening to their conversation whilst standing by the patio door.

"Have you ever seen one before, Grandma?" asked Alexander.

"I can't say I have. But then, I have often seen a rainbow and wondered if there really is a pot of gold at the end of it. As far as I know, there must be. People have often told me enough times that there is. Maybe I've always looked at the wrong end of the rainbow." Grandma replied.

I scratched my chin as though I'd had a thought. "You haven't seen a rainbow touchdown here lately have you?" I asked Alexander, pointing to where we had found our stash of coins.

"I don't believe that Granddad, you're making that up. You're telling porkies again."

"Making what up? Lies? I never lie. I only fib a little and only to your Grandma." I whispered knowing Grandmother was still standing by the patio door.

"But that's not true; there isn't a pot of gold at the end of a rainbow."

"Just a moment there young lad, how could you doubt me? Are you now telling me you don't believe in the Tooth Fairy, or Bill and Ben the Flower pot Men or Jack and the Beanstalk and the Goose that laid Golden Eggs?"

"No, of cause not, well yes, maybe the Tooth Fairy is true." Alexander admitted. "But that's only because I was left a pound under my pillow when I lost a milk tooth. The rest are only bedtime stories Daddy reads to me."

"Just because we don't always see something, it doesn't mean that it doesn't exist or isn't true."

"Yes." Said Alexander, a question in his voice and a look of not understanding on his face.

"Okay, let's do a little experiment, rub your hands together very hard." I told him.

"Why?"

"Don't ask questions, just do it." I instructed, showing him what I meant by rubbing my hands together.

After watching him for several seconds rubbing his hand together vigorously, I then asked,

"Did your hands get very warm?"

"Yes." He replied.

"But why was that, there was no fire, no source of heat, so how did it happen?"

"I don't know." He replied, but there was also a look of curiosity on his face a look of wanting to know.

"I will try to explain the best way I can. The heat is called friction. Friction is caused by two dry things rubbing together; with friction you can even light a fire just by rubbing two pieces of dried wood together. Your hands were dry, so they got hot, now do you understand?"

"Well yes, sort of." Alexander replied with a look of doubt.

"So let's study this tree. Do you think the rainbow could have ended here in the tree? Money must be coming from somewhere." I said looking up into the branches.

"I can't see anything up there other than that old bird's nest, Granddad."

"What? What birds nest? Yes I see, do you think the coins could be coming from that nest?"

"No."

"Why ever not?' I asked looking down at him. "It could be a magpie's or a jackdaws nest. These birds are known to collect shiny objects."

"But that nest is old and has fallen to bits." Said Alexander.

"Well then, that's more reason the contents have fallen to the ground. But I do agree, it does look a bit too old and these coins look new and clean."

"Yes, far too old." Alexander said, nodding and looking at on of the coins.

"Then maybe it's coming from your mother's herb garden?" I suggested.

"I don't think so Granddad." Responded Alexander shaking his head.

"Eureka, I've got it!" I exclaimed. 'The money is coming from your Mums herb garden; it's coming from the Mint."

"What?" Alexander said, his face distorted with grimace and puzzlement as though in pain.

'The money is coming from the Mint, that's where it's made." I told him.

"I don't think so, Granddad." Said Alexander, doubt and puzzlement was once more contorting his cheeky face.

'What? You doubt me again?" I asked, looking around to where I knew his father was preparing the barbecue for later. "Then ask your dad."

Alexander looked over to his father who was now on the patio, about to pick up a bag of charcoal for the barbecue and called out, "Dad, where does money come from?'

"My hard work." Was the chuckled reply.

"No seriously, where does it come from?"

"The bank, I guess, or mummy's purse."

"See Granddad," Alexander told me. "It comes from the bank."

"So ask him where the bank gets it." I urged. "Ask him where it's made?"

"Okay I will ask again." Said Alexander turning as though in a huff to look at his father, "Dad, where do they make money?"

"In the Mint." Replied Dad, still sorting through the charcoal bag for large lumps.

"You see," I told Alexander. "Now would I ever lie to you?"

'Yes, retorted Alexander, laughing.

"Later can we see if there's any more money in the Mint Granddad? "

"I don't think so Alexander, let's give it a rest for today." I suggested.

"Okay, Granddad." Said Alexander reluctantly. After seeing what his father was doing Alexander remarked. "Barbecue tonight Granddad and you know what that means?"

"Burnt sausages, blackened fingers and soiled teeth?" I said.

"No , Granddad, I think it's going to rain." Alexander said wistfully.

"What makes you think that? There's not a cloud in the sky."

"Didn't you hear it? I heard the distant rumble of thunder." He warned.

"No, no you didn't, that was my tummy. I'm so hungry that right now I could eat a horse."

"A horse?" questioned Alexander with a look of grimace on his face. "It could be in the sausages Granddad?" he said, a question of woe lingering on his words.

"Yes, but never mind that," I said, taking his hand, "Let's go and help Dad with the barbecue and annoy the neighbours with the stench of burning flesh and paraffin."

"Do you think Dad will rub two sticks together to light the barbecue?" he asked.

"I hope not, I'm starving." I said.

"Me too." Said Alexander.

"I think it best we give your dad a box of matches." I said grinning.

That day back in July, Alexander became a little richer, whilst I become a little poorer, but I didn't mind. After all, it's not only money that brings happiness.

© Dennis Pepper

My Lucky Stone

Chapter 1

Tired and dirty, I came in after playing outside. I took off my shoes only to find my father standing by the back door to the garden. He looked more confused than I had ever seen before.

"What on earth have you got in your pockets, my lad? Your shorts, they're half- way down to your ankles," he asked.

"Nothing..." I lied, edging my way into the living room.

"I doubt you have nothing," he said. "It looks like the elastic in your braces have snapped. But then, maybe you have what is known as the kitchen sink hidden in your pockets?"

He pulled and stretched my braces before letting them go with a snap.

"Ouch." I cried, and tried to run off, but no chance, Dad caught me.

"Come here you little scamp, and let your father give you a big cuddle and a sloppy wet kiss."

I tried to duck away but he grabbed me, lifted me high above his head, turned me up side down and shook me up and down like a yo-yo. I was unable to stop everything from falling out of my pockets, my marbles that bounced and rolled away on the living-room floor carpet, never to be seen again, my little hand-made catapult, constructed from elastic bands, a piece of chalk that I drew my hop-scotch square with, and a rusting nut and bolt I found in the park whilst walking home from school, and the thing most precious to me that had dropped to the floor was my lucky stone, a pebble with a hole right the way through it.

"Jumping cat-fish, is that all, no kitchen sink?" remarked Dad, his eyes scanning the contents of my pockets now scattered all over the floor.

"Yes Dad, that's all." I assured him whilst craning my head back to see where my treasures had fallen.

"But just wait a minute, haven't we forgotten something here?" he asked putting me gently back down on my feet.

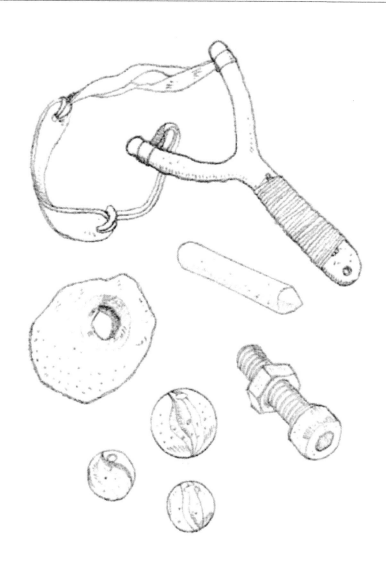

"No, I don't think so, I don't have anything else." I said somewhat disheartened, worried in thinking that these things on the floor would now be confiscated.

"Axe you sure?"

"Yes!" I replied, now feeling quite unsteady as the blood slowly flowed back away from my head to my feet.

"What about home-work? Are you not meant to be doing it before going out to play?"

"I've already done it." I replied smugly.

"What? You've already done it? That's impossible, I came home early today and you haven't come in from school until now."

"Well, that is, I did my homework during school break." I quickly informed him.

"What? What do you mean, during your school break?" he asked. "That's not homework, that's school work. Are you sure you've done it?"

"Yes, honestly, I've already done it."

"Okay. I believe you. Anyway, so long as you've done it and you've kept out of mischief its okay by me." He smiled ruffling up my hair. "Now be a good lad and pick up all that mess."

"From somewhere in the background there came the voice of my mother." Both of you, now wash your hands and lay the table please, dinner will be in ten minutes."

"Dad, can you see any of my marbles?" I asked.

"No, but 1 heard them rattling in your head earlier." He laughed, ruffling up my hair again.

'Never mind,' I thought, guessing the marbles had all disappeared under the settee or armchair. No doubt they will soon be sucked up into the vacuum cleaner and gone forever. But my main concern was finding my lucky stone, the one with a hole all the way through it.

This stone wasn't only lucky to me; it was a way of remembering things. At times I would blow through the hole at a certain angle and it would produce a weird sound, like wind howling through a broken window frame, or the slight gap beneath my bedroom door, or the sound of finger nails scraping down a blackboard. This would be enough to make you cringe and squeeze your teeth together.

I kept that stone for many, many years, and if I had forgotten something, all I needed to do was to squeeze my lucky stone and whatever it was that I had forgotten it would instantly come to mind.

Now where on earth did I put that stone?

© Dennis Pepper

Printed in Great Britain
by Amazon